Andrew Lang

Ban and arriere ban, a rally of fugitive rhymes

Second Edition

Andrew Lang

Ban and arriere ban, a rally of fugitive rhymes
Second Edition

ISBN/EAN: 9783337261894

Printed in Europe, USA, Canada, Australia, Japan

Cover: Foto ©Andreas Hilbeck / pixelio.de

More available books at **www.hansebooks.com**

BAN AND ARRIÈRE BAN

A RALLY OF

FUGITIVE RHYMES

Ban
and
arrière
Ban
by
Andrew
Lang

Ban and Arrière Ban

A RALLY OF FUGITIVE RHYMES

BY ANDREW LANG

Second Edition

LONDON

LONGMANS, GREEN & CO.

AND NEW YORK: 15 EAST 16TH STREET

1894

Edinburgh : T. and A. Constable, Printers to Her Majesty

TO

ELEANOR CHARLOTTE SELLAR

'Ban and Arrière Ban!' a host
   Broken, beaten, all unled,
They return as doth a ghost
   From the dead.

Sad or glad my rallied rhymes,
   Sought our dusty papers through,
For the sake of other times
   Come to you.

Times and places new we know,
   Faces fresh and seasons strange,
But the friends of long ago
   Do not change.

MANY of the verses in this collection have appeared in Magazines: 'How they held the Bass' was in 'Blackwood's Magazine; the 'Ballad of the Philanthropist' in 'Punch'; 'Calais Sands' in 'The Magazine of Art' (Messrs. Cassell and Co.); and others are recaptured from 'Longmans' Magazine,' 'Scribner's,' 'The Illustrated London News,' 'The English Illustrated Magazine,' 'Wit and Wisdom' (lines from Omar Khayyam), 'The St. James's Gazette,' and possibly other serials. Some pieces are from commendatory verses for books, as for Mr. Jacobs's 'Æsop'; some are from Mr. Rider Haggard's 'World's Desire,' and 'Cleopatra,' two are from Kirk's 'Secret Commonwealth' (Nutt, 1893), and 'Neiges d'Antan,' are from the author's 'Ballads and Lyrics of Old France,' now long out of print.

CONTENTS

III

POEMS WRITTEN UNDER THE INFLUENCE OF WORDSWORTH

CONTENTS

NEIGES D'ANTAN

BAN AND ARRIÈRE BAN

A SCOT TO JEANNE D'ARC

Dark Lily without blame,
Not upon us the shame,
Whose sires were to the Auld Alliance true,
They, by the Maiden's side,
Victorious fought and died,
One stood by thee that fiery torment through,
Till the White Dove from thy pure lips had
passed,
And thou wert with thine own St. Catherine at
the last.

Once only didst thou see
In artist's imagery,
Thine own face painted, and that precious thing
Was in an Archer's hand
From the leal Northern land.

A

A SCOT TO JEANNE D'ARC

Dark Lily without blame,
Not upon us the shame,
Whose sires were to the Auld Alliance true,
  They, by the Maiden's side,
  Victorious fought and died,
One stood by thee that fiery torment through,
  Till the White Dove from thy pure lips had
      passed,
And thou wert with thine own St. Catherine at
      the last.

  Once only didst thou see
  In artist's imagery,
Thine own face painted, and that precious thing
  Was in an Archer's hand
  From the leal Northern land.

A

Alas, what price would not thy people bring
  To win that portrait of the ruinous
Gulf of devouring years that hide the Maid from
      us !

    Born of a lowly line,
    Noteless as once was thine,
One of that name I would were kin to me,
    Who, in the Scottish Guard
    Won this for his reward,
To fight for France, and memory of thee :
  Not upon us, dark Lily without blame,
Not on the North may fall the shadow of that
      shame.

    On France and England both
    The shame of broken troth,
Of coward hate and treason black must be ;
    If England slew thee, France
    Sent not one word, one lance,
One coin to rescue or to ransom thee.
  And still thy Church unto the Maid denies
The halo and the palms, the Beatific prize.

But yet thy people calls
Within the rescued walls
Of Orleans ; and makes its prayer to thee ;
What though the Church have chidden
These orisons forbidden,
Yet art thou one of earth's immortal Three,
With him in Athens that of hemlock died,
And with thy Master dear whom the world cruci-
fied.

HOW THEY HELD THE BASS FOR KING JAMES—1691-1693

Time of Narrating—1743

YE hae heard Whigs crack o' the Saints in the
  Bass, my faith, a gruesome tale;
How the Remnant paid at a tippeny rate, for a
  quart o' ha'penny ale!
But I'll tell ye anither tale o' the Bass, that'll
  hearten ye up to hear,
Sae I pledge ye to Middleton first in a glass, and
  a health to the Young Chevalier!

The Bass stands frae North Berwick Law a
  league or less to sea,
About its feet the breakers beat, abune the sea-
  maws flee,
There's castle stark and dungeon dark, wherein
  the godly lay,

4

That made their rant for the Covenant through
    mony a weary day.
For twal' years lang the caverns rang wi' preaching,
    prayer, and psalm,
Ye'd think the winds were soughing wild, when
    a' the winds were calm,
There wad they preach, each Saint to each, and
    glower as the soldiers pass,
And Peden wared his malison on a bonny leaguer
    lass,
As she stood and daffed, while the warders
    laughed, and wha sae blithe as she,
But a wind o' ill worked his warlock will, and
    flang her out to sea.
Then wha sae bright as the Saints that night,
    and an angel came, say they,
And sang in the cell where the Righteous dwell,
    but he took na a Saint away.
There yet might they be, for nane could flee, and
    nane daur'd break the jail,
And still the sobbing o' the sea might mix wi'
    their warlock wail,

But then came in black echty-echt, and bluidy
    echty-nine,

Wi' Cess, and Press, and Presbytery, and a' the
    dule sin' syne,

The Saints won free wi' the power o' the key,
    and cavaliers maun pine!

It was Halyburton, Middleton, and Roy and
    young Dunbar,

That Livingstone took on Cromdale haughs, in
    the last fight of the war:

And they were warded in the Bass, till the time
    they should be slain,

Where bluidy Mitchell, and Blackader, and
    Earlston lang had lain;

Four lads alone, 'gainst a garrison, but Glory
    crowns their names,

For they brought it to pass that they took the
    Bass, and they held it for King James!

It isna by preaching half the night, ye'll burst
    a dungeon door,

It wasna by dint o' psalmody they broke the
    hold, they four,
For lang years three that rock in the sea bade
    Wullie Wanbeard gae swing,
And England and Scotland fause may be, but
    the Bass Rock stands for the King!

There's but ae pass gangs up the Bass, it's
    guarded wi' strong gates four,
And still as the soldiers went to the sea, they
    steikit them, door by door,
And this did they do when they helped a crew
    that brought their coals on shore.
Thither all had gone, save three men alone: then
    Middleton gripped his man,
Halyburton felled the sergeant lad, Dunbar seized
    the gunner, Swan;
Roy bound their hands, in hempen bands, and the
    Cavaliers were free.
And they trained the guns on the soldier loons
    that were down wi' the boat by the sea!

Then Middleton cried frae the high cliff-side,
    and his voice garr'd the auld rocks ring,
'Will ye stand or flee by the land or sea, for I
    hold the Bass for the King ?'

They had nae desire to face the fire ; it was mair
    than men might do,
So they e'en sailed back in the auld coal-smack, a
    sorry and shame-faced crew,
And they hirpled doun to Edinburgh toun, wi'
    the story of their shames,
How the prisoners bold had broken hold, and
    kept the Bass for King James.

King James he has sent them guns and men, and
    the Whigs they guard the Bass,
But they never could catch the Cavaliers, who
    took toll of ships that pass,
They fared wild and free as the birds o' the sea,
    and at night they went on the wing,
And they lifted the kye o' Whigs far and nigh,
    and they revelled and drank to the King.

Then Wullie Wanbeard sends his ships to siege
    the Bass in form,
And first shall they break the fortress down, and
    syne the Rock they 'll storm.
After twa days' fight they fled in the night, and
    glad eneuch to go,
With their rigging rent, and their powder spent,
    and many a man laid low.

So for lang years three did they sweep the sea,
    but a closer watch was set,
Till nae food had they, but twa ounce a day o'
    meal was the maist they 'd get.
And men fight but tame on an empty wame, so
    they sent a flag o' truce,
And blithe were the Privy Council then, when the
    Whigs had heard that news.
Twa Lords they sent wi' a strang intent to be
    dour on each Cavalier,
But wi' French cakes fine, and his last drap o'
    wine, did Middleton make them cheer,

On the muzzles o' guns he put coats and caps,
    and he set them aboot the wa's,
And the Whigs thocht then he had food and men
    to stand for the Rightfu' Cause.
So he got a' he craved, and his men were saved,
    and nane might say them nay,
Wi' sword by si'le, and flag o' pride, free men
    might they gang their way,
They might fare to France, they might bide at
    hame, and the better their grace to buy,
Wullie Wanbeard's purse maun pay the keep o'
    the men that did him defy !

Men never hae gotten sic terms o' peace since
    first men went to war,
As got Halyburton, and Middleton, and Roy, and
    the young Dunbar.
Sae I drink to ye here, *To the Young Chevalier !* I
    hae said ye an auld man's say,
And there may hae been mightier deeds of arms,
    but there never was nane sae gay !

THREE PORTRAITS OF PRINCE CHARLES

1731

BEAUTIFUL face of a child,
  Lighted with laughter and glee,
Mirthful, and tender, and wild,
  My heart is heavy for thee !

1744

Beautiful face of a youth,
  As an eagle poised to fly forth,
To the old land loyal of truth,
  To the hills and the sounds of the North :
Fair face, daring and proud,
  Lo ! the shadow of doom, even now,
The fate of thy line, like a cloud,
  Rests on the grace of thy brow !

11

1773

Cruel and angry face,
  Hateful and heavy with wine,
Where are the gladness, the grace,
  The beauty, the mirth that were thine ?

Ah, my Prince, it were well,—
  Hadst thou to the gods been dear,—
To have fallen where Keppoch fell,
  With the war-pipe loud in thine ear !
To have died with never a stain
  On the fair White Rose of Renown,
To have fallen, fighting in vain,
  For thy father, thy faith, and thy crown !
More than thy marble pile,
  With its women weeping for thee,
Were to dream in thine ancient isle,
  To the endless dirge of the sea !
But the Fates deemed otherwise,
  Far thou sleepest from home,
From the tears of the Northern skies,
  In the secular dust of Rome.

A city of death and the dead,
    But thither a pilgrim came,
Wearing on weary head
    The crowns of years and fame :
Little the Lucrine lake
    Or Tivoli said to him,
Scarce did the memories wake
    Of the far-off years and dim.
For he stood by Avernus' shore,
    But he dreamed of a Northern glen
And he murmured, over and o'er,
    For Charlie and his men :
And his feet, to death that went,
    Crept forth to St. Peter's shrine,
And the latest Minstrel bent
    O'er the last of the Stuart line.

FROM OMAR KHAYYAM

RHYMED FROM THE PROSE VERSION OF
MR. JUSTIN HUNTLY M'CARTHY

THE Paradise they bid us fast to win
Hath Wine and Women ; is it then a sin
   To live as we shall live in Paradise,
And make a Heaven of Earth, ere Heaven begin ?

The wise may search the world from end to end,
From dusty nook to dusty nook, my friend,
   And nothing better find than girls and wine,
Of all the things they neither make nor mend.

Nay, listen thou who, walking on Life's way,
Hast seen no lovelock of thy love's grow grey
   Listen, and love thy life, and let the Wheel
Of Heaven go spinning its own wilful way.
  14

Man is a flagon, and his soul the wine,
Man is a lamp, wherein the Soul doth shine,
  Man is a shaken reed, wherein that wind,
The Soul, doth ever rustle and repine.

Each morn I say, to-night I will repent,
Repent! and each night go the way I went—
  The way of Wine; but now that reigns the
    rose,
Lord of Repentance, rage not, but relent.

I wish to drink of wine—so deep, so deep—
The scent of wine my sepulchre shall steep,
  And they, the revellers by Omar's tomb,
Shall breathe it, and in Wine shall fall asleep.

Before the rent walls of a ruined town
Lay the King's skull, whereby a bird flew down
  'And where,' he sang, 'is all thy clash of arms?
Where the sonorous trumps of thy renown?'

ÆSOP

He sat among the woods, he heard
  The sylvan merriment : he saw
The pranks of butterfly and bird,
  The humours of the ape, the daw.

And in the lion or the frog—
  In all the life of moor and fen,
In ass and peacock, stork and dog,
  He read similitudes of men.

'Of these, from those,' he cried, 'we come,
  Our hearts, our brains descend from these.'
And lo ! the Beasts no more were dumb,
  But answered out of brakes and trees :

'Not ours,' they cried ; ' Degenerate,
  If ours at all,' they cried again,
16

‘ Ye fools, who war with God and Fate,
  Who strive and toil : strange race of men.

‘ For *we* are neither bond nor free,
  For *we* have neither slaves nor kings,
But near to Nature's heart are we,
  And conscious of her secret things.

‘ Content are we to fall asleep,
  And well content to wake no more,
We do not laugh, we do not weep,
  Nor look behind us and before ;

But were there cause for moan or mirth,
  'Tis *we*, not you, should sigh or scorn,
Oh, latest children of the Earth,
  Most childish children Earth has borne.'

.   .   .   .   .

They spoke, but that misshapen slave
  Told never of the thing he heard,
And unto men their portraits gave,
  In likenesses of beast and bird !

B

LES ROSES DE SÂDI

THIS morning I vowed I would bring thee my
    Roses,
They were thrust in the band that my bodice
    encloses,
But the breast-knots were broken, the Roses went
    free.

The breast-knots were broken; the Roses
    together
Floated forth on the wings of the wind and the
    weather,
And they drifted afar down the streams of the
    sea.

And the sea was as red as when sunset uncloses,
But my raiment is sweet from the scent of the
    Roses,
Thou shalt know, Love, how fragrant a memory
    can be.

18

THE HAUNTED TOWER

SUGGESTED BY A POEM OF THÉOPHILE GAUTIER

IN front he saw the donjon tall
    Deep in the woods, and stayed to scan
The guards that slept along the wall,
    Or dozed upon the bartizan.
He marked the drowsy flag that hung
    Unwaved by wind, unfrayed by shower,
He listened to the birds that sung
    Go forth and win the haunted tower !
The tangled brake made way for him,
    The twisted brambles bent aside ;
And lo, he pierced the forest dim,
    And lo, he won the fairy bride !
For *he* was young, but ah ! we find,
    All we, whose beards are flecked with grey,
Our fairy castle 's far behind,
    We watch it from the darkling way :

19

'Twas ours, that palace, in our youth,
　　We revelled there in happy cheer :
Who scarce dare visit now in sooth,
　　Le Vieux Château de Souvenir !
For not the boughs of forest green
　　Begird that castle far away,
There is a mist where we have been
　　That weeps about it, cold and grey.
And if we seek to travel back
　　'Tis through a thicket dim and sere,
With many a grave beside the track,
　　And many a haunting form of fear.
Dead leaves are wet among the moss,
　　With weed and thistle overgrown—
A ruined barge within the fosse,
　　A castle built of crumbling stone !
The drawbridge drops from rusty chains,
　　There comes no challenge from the hold ;
No squire, nor dame, nor knight remains,
　　Of all who dwelt with us of old.
And there is silence in the hall
　　No sound of songs, no ray of fire ;

But gloom where all was glad, and all
    Is darkened with a vain desire.
And every picture's fading fast,
    Of fair Jehanne, or Cydalise.
Lo, the white shadows hurrying past,
    Below the boughs of dripping trees!

.   .   .   .

Ah rise, and march, and look not back,
    Now the long way has brought us here;
We may not turn and seek the track
    To the old Château de Souvenir!

BOAT-SONG

ADRIFT, with starlit skies above,
 With starlit seas below,
We move with all the suns that move
 With all the seas that flow :
For, bond or free, earth, sky, and sea
 Wheel with one central will,
And thy heart drifteth on to me,
 And only Time stands still.

Between two shores of death we drift,
 Behind are things forgot,
Before, the tide is racing swift
 To shores man knoweth not.
Above, the sky is far and cold,
 Below, the moaning sea
Sweeps o'er the loves that were of old,
 But thou, Love, love thou me.

22

Ah, lonely are the ocean ways,
  And dangerous the deep,
And frail the fairy barque that strays
  Above the seas asleep.
Ah, toil no more with helm or oar,
  We drift, or bond or free,
On yon far shore the breakers roar,
  But thou, Love, love thou me !

LOST LOVE

Who wins his Love shall lose her,
  Who loses her shall gain,
For still the spirit woos her,
  A soul without a stain ;
And Memory still pursues her
  With longings not in vain !

He loses her who gains her,
  Who watches day by day
The dust of time that stains her,
  The griefs that leave her grey,
The flesh that yet enchains her
  Whose grace hath passed away !

Oh, happier he who gains not
  The Love some seem to gain :

24

The joy that custom stains not
  Shall still with him remain,
The loveliness that wanes not,
  The Love that ne'er can wane.

In dreams she grows not older
  The lands of Dream among,
Though all the world wax colder,
  Though all the songs be sung,
In dreams doth he behold her
  Still fair and kind and young.

THE PROMISE OF HELEN

Whom hast thou longed for most,
  True love of mine?
Whom hast thou loved and lost?
  Lo, she is thine!

She that another wed
  Breaks from her vow;
She that hath long been dead
  Wakes for thee now.

Dreams haunt the hapless bed,
  Ghosts haunt the night,
Life crowns her living head,
  Love and Delight.

Nay, not a dream nor ghost,
  Nay, but Divine,
She that was loved and lost
  Waits to be thine!

THE RESTORATION OF ROMANCE

TO H. R. H., R. L. S., A. C. D., AND S. W.

KING ROMANCE was wounded deep,
   All his knights were dead and gone,
All his court was fallen on sleep,
   In a vale of Avalon !
Nay, men said, he will not come,
   Any night or any morn.
Nay, his puissant voice is dumb,
   Silent his enchanted horn !

King Romance was forfeited,
   Banished from his Royal home,
With a price upon his head,
   Driven with sylvan folk to roam.
King Romance is fallen, banned,
   Cried his foemen overbold,
Broken is the wizard wand,
   All the stories have been told !

Then you came from South and North,
　　From Tugela, from the Tweed,
Blazoned his achievements forth,
　　King Romance is come indeed !
All his foes are overthrown,
　　All their wares cast out in scorn,
King Romance hath won his own,
　　And the lands where he was born !

Marsac at adventure rides,
　　Felon men meet felon scathe,
Micah Clarke is taking sides
　　For King Monmouth and the Faith ;
For a Cause or for a lass
　　Men are willing to be slain,
And the dungeons of the Bass
　　Hold a prisoner again.

King Romance with wand of gold
　　Sways the realms he ruled of yore.
Hills Dalgetty roamed of old,
　　Valleys of enchanted Kôr :

Waves his sceptre o'er the isles,
   Claims the pirates' treasuries,
Through innumerable miles
   Of the siren-haunted seas !

Elfin folk of coast and cave,
   Laud him in the woven dance,
All the tribes of wold and wave
   Bow the knee to King Romance !
Wand'ring voices Chaucer knew
   On the mountain and the main,
Cry the haunted forest through,
   King Romance has come again !

CENTRAL AMERICAN ANTIQUITIES

IN SOUTH KENSINGTON MUSEUM

'YOUTH and crabbed age
    Cannot live together;'
        So they say.
On this little page
    See you when and whether
        That they may.

Age was very old—
    Stones from Chichimec
        Hardly wrung;
Youth had hair of gold
    Knotted on her neck—
        Fair and young!

Age was carved with odd
    Slaves, and priests that slew them—
        God and Beast;

Man and Beast and God—
  There she sat and drew them,
    King and Priest!

There she sat and drew
  Many a monstrous head
    And antique :
Horrors from Peru,
  Huacas doubly dead,
    Dead cacique!

Ere Pizarro came
  These were lords of men
    Long ago ;
Gods without a name,
  Born or how or when,
    None may know!

Now from Yucatan
  These doth Science bear
    Over seas ;
And methinks a man
  Finds youth doubly fair,
    Sketching these !

ON CALAIS SANDS

On Calais Sands the grey began,
  Then rosy red above the grey,
The morn with many a scarlet van
  Leap'd, and the world was glad with May!
The little waves along the bay
  Broke white upon the shelving strands;
The sea-mews flitted white as they
      On Calais Sands!

On Calais Sands must man with man
  Wash honour clean in blood to-day;
On spaces wet from waters wan
  How white the flashing rapiers play,
Parry, riposte! and lunge! The fray
  Shifts for a while, then mournful stands
The Victor: life ebbs fast away
      On Calais Sands!

32

On Calais Sands a little space
   Of silence, then the plash and spray,
The sound of eager waves that ran
   To kiss the perfumed locks astray,
To touch these lips that ne'er said 'Nay,'
   To dally with the helpless hands ;
Till the deep sea in silence lay
      On Calais Sands !

Between the lilac and the may
   She waits her love from alien lands
Her love is colder than the clay
      On Calais Sands !

C

BALLADE OF YULE

This life's most jolly, Amiens said,
　　Heigh-ho, the Holly !   So sang he.
As the good Duke was comforted
　　In forest exile, so may we !
The years may darken as they flee,
　　And Christmas bring his melancholy :
But round the old mahogany tree
　　We drink, we sing *Heigh-ho, the Holly !*

Though some are dead and some are fled
　　To lands of summer over sea,
The holly berry keeps his red,
　　The merry children keep their glee ;
They hoard with artless secresy
　　This gift for Maude, and that for Molly,
And Santa Claus he turns the key
　　On Christmas Eve, *Heigh-ho, the Holly !*
34

Amid the snow the birds are fed,
  The snow lies deep on lawn and lea,
The skies are shining overhead,
  The robin's tame that was so free.
Far North, at home, the 'barley bree'
  They brew; they give the hour to folly,
How 'Rab and Allan cam to pree,'
  They sing, we sing *Heigh-ho, the Holly!*

ENVOI

Friend, let us pay the wonted fee,
  The yearly tithe of mirth: be jolly!
It is a duty so to be,
  Though half we sigh, *Heigh-ho, the Holly!*

POSCIMUR

FROM HORACE

Hush, for they call!   If in the shade,
My lute, we twain have idly strayed,
And song for many a season made,
   Once more reply ;
Once more we'll play as we have played,
   My lute and I !

Roman the song : the strain you know,
The Lesbian wrought it long ago.
Now singing as he charged the foe,
   Now in the bay,
Where safe in the shore-water's flow
   His galleys lay.

So sang he Bacchus and the Nine,
And Venus and her boy divine,

And Lycus of the dusky eyne,
        The dusky hair ;
So shalt thou sing, ah, Lute of mine,
        Of all things fair ;

Apollo's glory ! Sounding shell,
Thou lute, to Jove desirable,
When soft thine accents sigh and swell
        At festival—
Delight more dear than words can tell,
        Attend my call !

ON HIS DEAD SEA-MEW

FROM THE GREEK

I

Bird of the graces, dear sea-mew, whose note
    Was like the halcyon's song,
In death thy wings and thy sweet spirit float
    Still paths of the night along !

II

THE SAILOR'S GRAVE

Tomb of a shipwrecked seafarer am I,
    But thou, sail on !
For homeward safe did other vessels fly,
    Though we were gone.

FROM MELEAGER

I LOVE not the wine-cup, but if thou art fain
 I should drink, do thou taste it, and bring it to
  me ;
If it touch but thy lips it were hard to refrain,
 It were hard from the sweet maid who bears it
  to flee ;
For the cup ferries over the kisses, and plain
 Does it speak of the grace that was given it by
  thee.

39

ON THE GARLAND SENT TO RHODOCLEIA

RUFINUS

GOLDEN EYES

'AH, Golden Eyes, to win you yet,
I bring mine April coronet,
The lovely blossoms of the spring,
For you I weave, to you I bring
These roses with the lilies set,
The dewy dark-eyed violet,
Narcissus, and the wind-flower wet :
Wilt thou disdain mine offering ?
     Ah, Golden Eyes !

Crowned with thy lover's flowers, forget
The pride wherein thy heart is set,
For thou, like these or anything,
Hast but a moment of thy spring,
Thy spring, and then—the long regret !
     Ah, Golden Eyes !'

A GALLOWAY GARLAND

WE know not, on these hills of ours,
   The fabled asphodel of Greece,
That filleth with immortal flowers
   Fields where the heroes are at peace !
   Not ours are myrtle buds like these
That breathe o'er isles where memories dwell
   Of Sappho, in enchanted seas !

We meet not, on our upland moor,
   The singing Maid of Helicon,
You may not hear her music pure
   Float on the mountain meres withdrawn ;
   The Muse of Greece, the Muse is gone !
But we have songs that please us well
   And flowers we love to look upon.

More sweet than Southern myrtles far
   The bruised Marsh-myrtle breatheth keen ;

41

Parnassus names the flower, the star,
  That shines among the well-heads green
  The bright Marsh-asphodels between—
Marsh-myrtle and Marsh-asphodel
  May crown the Northern Muse a queen!

CELIA'S EYES

TELL me not that babies dwell
   In the deeps of Celia's eyes;
Cupid in each hazel well
   Scans his beauties with surprise,
      And would, like Narcissus, drown
      In my Celia's eyes of brown.

Tell me not that any goes
   Safe by that enchanted place;
Eros dwells with Anteros
   In the garden of her Face,
      Where like friends who late were foes
      Meet the white and crimson Rose.

BRITANNIA

FROM JULES LEMAÎTRE

THY mouth is fresh as cherries on the bough,
  Red cherries in the dawning, and more white
Than milk or white camellias is thy brow;
  And as the golden corn below the might
  Of mellow August suns, thy hair is bright,
The corn that drinks the Sun's less fair than thou;
While through thine eyes the child-soul gazeth
    now—
  Eyes like the flower that was Rousseau's delight.

Sister of sad Ophelia, say, shall these
Thy pearly teeth grow like piano keys
  Yellow and long; while thou, all skin and bone,
Angles and morals, in a sky-blue veil,
Shalt hosts of children to the sermon hale,
  Blare hymns, read chapters, backbite, and
    intone?

GALLIA

LADY, lady neat
  Of the roguish eye,
    Wherefore dost thou hie,
Stealthy, down the street,
On well-booted feet ?
  From French novels I
    Gather that you fly,
Guy or Jules to meet.

Furtive dost thou range,
Oft thy cab dost change ;
  So, at least, 'tis said :
Oh, the sad old tale
Passionately stale,
  We've so often read !

THE FAIRY MINISTER

The Rev. Mr. Kirk of Aberfoyle was carried away by the
Fairies in 1692.

PEOPLE of Peace! a peaceful man,
  Well worthy of your love was he,
Who, while the roaring Garry ran
  Red with the life-blood of Dundee,
While coats were turning, crowns were falling,
  Wandered along his valley still,
And heard your mystic voices calling
  From fairy knowe and haunted hill.
He heard, he saw, he knew too well
  The secrets of your fairy clan;
You stole him from the haunted dell,
  Who never more was seen of man.
Now far from heaven, and safe from hell,
  Unknown of earth, he wanders free.

Would that he might return and tell
  Of his mysterious Company !
For we have tired the Folk of Peace ;
  No more they tax our corn and oil ;
Their dances on the moorland cease,
  The Brownie stints his wonted toil.
No more shall any shepherd meet
  The ladies of the fairy clan,
Nor are their deathly kisses sweet
  On lips of any earthly man.
And half I envy him who now,
  Clothed in her Court's enchanted green,
By moonlit loch or mountain's brow
  Is Chaplain to the Fairy Queen.

TO ROBERT LOUIS STEVENSON

WITH KIRK'S 'SECRET COMMONWEALTH'

O Louis! you that like them maist,
Ye 're far frae kelpie, wraith, and ghaist,
And fairy dames, no unco chaste,
    And haunted cell.
Among a heathen clan ye 're placed,
    That kensna hell!

Ye hae nae heather, peat, nor birks,
Nae trout in a' yer burnies lurks,
There are nae bonny U.P. kirks,
    An awfu' place!
Nane kens the Covenant o' Works
    Frae that o' Grace!

But whiles, maybe, to them ye 'll read
Blads o' the Covenanting creed,
And whiles their pagan wames ye 'll feed
    On halesome parritch;

And syne ye 'll gar them learn a screed
  O' the Shorter Carritch.

Yet thae uncovenanted shavers
Hae rowth, ye say, o' clash and clavers
O' gods and etins—auld wives' havers,
   But their delight ;
The voice o' him that tells them quavers
   Just wi' fair fright.

And ye might tell, ayont the faem,
Thae Hieland clashes o' our hame
To speak the truth, I takna shame
   To half believe them ;
And, stamped wi' *Tusitala's* name,
   They 'll a' receive them.

And folk to come ayont the sea
May hear the yowl o' the Banshie
And frae the water-kelpie flee,
   Ere a' things cease,
And island bairns may stolen be
   By the Folk o' Peace.

D

FOR MARK TWAIN'S JUBILEE

To brave Mark Twain, across the sea,
The years have brought his jubilee ;
   One hears it half with pain,
That fifty years have passed and gone
Since danced the merry star that shone
   Above the babe, Mark Twain !

How many and many a weary day,
When sad enough were we, 'Mark's way
   (Unlike the Laureate's Mark's)
Has made us laugh until we cried,
And, sinking back exhausted, sighed,
   Like Gargery, *Wot larx !*

We turn his pages, and we see
The Mississippi flowing free ;
   We turn again, and grin

O'er all *Tom Sawyer* did and planned,
With him of the Ensanguined Hand,
   With *Huckleberry Finn !*

Spirit of mirth, whose chime of bells
Shakes on his cap, and sweetly swells
   Across the Atlantic main,
Grant that Mark's laughter never die,
That men, through many a century,
   May chuckle o'er Mark Twain !

III

POEMS

WRITTEN UNDER

THE INFLUENCE OF

WORDSWORTH

[Intelligent Reviewers are prayed to note that of these poems there be here found no more than *three*.]

MIST

Mist, though I love thee not, who puttest down
   Trout in the Lochs, (they feed not, as a rule,
   At least on fly, in mere or river-pool
When fogs have fallen, and the air is lown,
And on each Ben, a pillow not a crown,
   The fat folds rest,) thou, Mist, hast power to cool
   The blatant declamations of the fool
Who raves reciting through the heather brown.

Much do I bar the matron, man, or lass
   Who cries ' How lovely!' and who does not spare
When light and shadow on the mountain pass,—
   Shadow and light, and gleams exceeding fair,
O'er rock, and glade, and glen,—to shout, the Ass,
   To me, to me the Poet, ' Oh, look there !'

LINES

Written under the influence of Wordsworth, with a
slate-pencil on a window of the dining-room at the
Lowood Hotel, Windermere, while waiting for tea, after
being present at the Grasmere Sports on a very wet day,
and in consequence of a recent perusal of *Belinda*, a
Novel, by Miss Broughton, whose absence is regretted.

How solemn is the front of this Hotel,
　　When now the hills are swathed in modest mist,
And none can speak of scenery, nor tell
　　Of 'tints of amber,' or of 'amethyst.'
Here once thy daughters, young Romance, did
　　　　dwell,
　　Here *Sara* flirted with whoever list,
Belinda loved not wisely but too well,
　　And *Mr. Ford* played the Philologist !
　　56

Haunted the house is, and the balcony
  Where that fond Matron knew her Lover near,
And here we sit, and wait for tea, and sigh,
  While the sad rain sobs in the sullen mere,
And all our hearts go forth into the cry,
  Would that the teller of the tale were here !

LINES

Written on the window pane of a railway carriage after reading an advertisement of sunlight soap, and *Poems*, by William Wordsworth.

I PASSED upon the wings of Steam
    Along Tay's valley fair,
The book I read had such a theme
    As bids the Soul despair.

A tale of miserable men
    Of hearts with doubt distraught,
Wherein a melancholy pen
    With helpless problems fought.

Where many a life was brought to dust,
    And many a heart laid low,
And many a love was smirched with lust—
    I raised mine eyes, and, oh !—

I marked upon a common wall,
   These simple words of hope,
That mute appeal to one and all,
   Cheer up ! Use Sunlight Soap !

Our moral energies have range
   Beyond their seeming scope,
How tonic were the words, how strange,
   Cheer up ! Use Sunlight Soap !

'Behold,' I cried, 'the inner touch
   That lifts the Soul through cares !
I loved that Soap-boiler so much
   I blessed him unawares !

Perchance he is some vulgar man,
   Engrossed in £ s. d.
But, ah ! through Nature's holy plan
   He whispered hope to me !

ODE TO GOLF

'Delusive Nymph, farewell!'
    How oft we 've said or sung,
When balls evasive fell,
Or in the jaws of 'Hell,'
    Or salt sea-weeds among,
'Mid shingle and sea-shell!

How oft beside the Burn,
    We play the sad 'two more';
How often at the turn,
The heather must we spurn;
    How oft we 've 'topped and swore,'
In bent and whin and fern!

Yes, when the broken head
    Bounds further than the ball,
The heart has inly bled.

61

Ah ! and the lips have said
   Words we would fain recall—
Wild words, of passion bred !

In bunkers all unknown,
   Far beyond 'Walkinshaw,
Where never ball had flown—
Reached by ourselves alone—
   Caddies have heard with awe
The music of our moan !

Yet, Nymph, if once alone,
   The ball hath featly fled—
Not smitten from the bone—
That drive doth still atone ;
   And one long shot laid dead
Our grief to the winds hath blown !

So, still beside the tee,
   We meet in storm or calm,
Lady, and worship thee ;
While the loud lark sings free,
   Piping his matin psalm
Above the grey sad sea !

FRESHMAN'S TERM

RETURN again, thou Freshman's year,
 When bloom was on the rye,
When breakfast came with bottled beer,
 When Pleasure walked the High;
When Torpid Bumps were more by far
 To every opening mind
Than Trade, or Shares, or Peace, or War,
 To senior humankind;
When ribbons of outrageous hues
 Were worn with honest pride,
When much was talked of boats and crews,
 When Proctors were defied:
When Tick was in its early bloom,
 When Schools were far away,
As vaguely distant as the tomb,
 Nor more regarded—they!

When arm was freely linked with arm
　　Beneath the College limes,
When Sunday grinds possessed a charm
　　Denied to *College Rhymes*:
When ices were in much request
　　Beside the April fire,
When men were very strangely dressed
　　By Standen or by Prior.
Return, ye Freshman's Terms! They *do*
　　Return, and much the same,
To boys, who, just like me and you,
　　Play the absurd old game!

A TOAST

Kate Kennedy is the Patron Saint of St. Leonard's and St.
Salvator.   Her history is quite unknown.

THE learned are all ' in a swither,'
    (They don't very often agree,)
They know not her ' whence ' nor her ' whither,'
The Maiden we drink to together,
    The College's Kate Kennedie !

Did she shine in days early or later ?
    Did she ever achieve a degree ?
Was she pretty or plain ?   Did she mate, or
Live lonely ?   And who was the *pater*
    Of mystical Kate Kennedie ?

The learned may scorn her and scout her,
    But true to her colours are *we*,

E

The learned may mock her and flout her,
But surely we'll rally about her,
    In the College that stands by the Sea !

So here's to her memory ! here to
    The mystical Maiden drink we,
We pledge her, and we'll persevere too,
Though the reason is not very clear to
    The critical mind, nor to *me*.
Here's to Kate ! she's our own, and she's dear to
    The College that stands by the Sea.

DEATH IN JUNE

FOR CRICKETERS ONLY

June is the month of Suicides

'WHY do we slay ourselves in June,
　　When life, if ever, seems so sweet?
When "Moon," and "tune," and "afternoon,"
　　And other happy rhymes we meet,
When strawberries are coming soon?
　　Why do we do it?' you repeat!

Ah, careless butterfly, to thee
　　The strawberry seems passing good;
And sweet, on Music's wings, to flee
　　Amid the waltzing multitude,
And revel late—perchance till three—
　　For Love is monarch of thy mood!

67

Alas ! to *us* no solace shows
    For sorrows we endure—at Lord's,
When Oxford's bowling *always* goes
    For 'fours,' for ever to the cords—
Or more, perhaps, with 'overthrows';—
    These things can pierce the heart like swords !

And thus it is though woods are green,
    Though mayflies down the Test are rolling,
Though sweet, the silver showers between,
    The finches sing in strains consoling,
We cut our throats for very spleen,
    And very shame of Oxford's bowling !

TO CORRESPONDENTS

My Postman, though I fear thy tread,
   And tremble as thy foot draws nearer,
'Tis not the Christmas Dun I dread,
   My mortal foe is much severer,—
The Unknown Correspondent, who,
   With undefatigable pen,
And nothing in the world to do,
   Perplexes literary men.

From Pentecost and Ponder's End
   They write : from Deal, and from Dacotah,
The people of the Shetlands send
   No inconsiderable quota ;
They write for *autographs* ; in vain,
   In vain does Phyllis write, and Flora,
They write that *Allan Quatermain*
   Is not at all the book for Brora.

69

They write to say that 'they have met
    This writer · at a garden party,
And though' this writer '*may* forget,'
    Their recollection's keen and hearty.
' And will you praise in your reviews
    A novel by our distant cousin ? '
These letters from Provincial Blues
    Assail us daily by the dozen !

O friends with time upon your hands,
    O friends with postage-stamps in plenty,
O poets out of many lands,
    O youths and maidens under twenty,
Seek out some other wretch to bore,
    Or wreak yourselves upon your neighbours,
And leave me to my dusty lore
    And my unprofitable labours !

BALLADE OF DIFFICULT RHYMES

WITH certain rhymes 'tis hard to deal;
  For 'silver' we have ne'er a rhyme.
On 'orange' (as on orange peel)
  The bard has slipped full many a time.
With 'babe' there 's scarce a sound will chime,
  Though 'astrolabe' fits like a glove;
But, ye that on Parnassus climb,
  Why, why are rhymes so rare to *Love*?

A rhyme to 'cusp,' to beg or steal,
  I 've sought, from evensong to prime,
But vain is my poetic zeal,
  There 's not one sound is worth a 'dime':
'Bilge,' 'coif,' 'scarf,' 'window'—deeds of crime
  I 'd do to gain the rhymes thereof;
Nor shrink from acts of moral grime—
  Why, why are rhymes so rare to *Love*?

To 'dove' my fancies flit, and wheel
   Like butterflies on banks of thyme.
'Above'?—or 'shove'?—alas!   I feel,
   They're too much used to be sublime.
I scorn with angry pantomime,
   The thought of 'move' (pronounced as *muv*).
Ah, in Apollo's golden clime
   Why, why are rhymes so rare to *Love* ?

ENVOI

Prince of the lute and lyre, reveal
   New rhymes, fresh minted, from above,
Nor still be deaf to our appeal.
   Why, *why* are rhymes so rare to *Love* ?

BALLANT O' BALLANTRAE

TO ROBERT LOUIS STEVENSON

Written in wet weather, this conveyed to the Master of
Ballantrae a wrong idea of a very beautiful and charming
place, with links, a river celebrated by Burns, good sea-
fishing, and, on the river, a ruined castle at every turn of
the stream. 'Try Ballantrae' is a word of wisdom.

WHAN suthern wunds gar spindrift flee
Abune the clachan, faddums hie,
Whan for the cluds I canna see
   The bonny lift,
I 'd fain indite an Ode to *thee*
   Had I the gift!

Ken ye the coast o' wastland Ayr?
Oh mon, it 's unco bleak and bare!
Ye daunder here, ye daunder there,
   And mak' your moan,
They 've rain and wund eneuch to tear
   The suthern cone!

Ye 're seekin' sport !   There 's nane ava',
Ye 'll sit and glower ahint the wa'
At bleesin' breakers till ye staw,
  If that 's yer wush ;
'There 's aye the Stinchar.'   Hoot awa',
  She wunna fush !

She wunna fush at ony gait,
She 's roarin' reid in wrathfu' spate ;
Maist like yer kimmer when ye 're late
  Frae Girvan Fair !
Forbye to speer for leave I 'm blate
  For fushin' there !

O Louis, you that writes in Scots,
Ye 're far awa' frae stirks and stots,
Wi' drookit hurdies, tails in knots,
  An unco way !
My mirth 's like thorns aneth the pots
  In Ballantrae !

SONG BY THE SUB-CONSCIOUS SELF

RHYMES MADE IN A DREAM

I KNOW not what my secret is,
 I know but it is mine ;
I know to dwell with it were bliss,
 To die for it divine.
I cannot yield it in a kiss,
 Nor breathe it in a sigh.
I know that I have lived for this ;
 For this, my love, I die.

THE HAUNTED HOMES OF ENGLAND

THE Haunted Homes of England,
   How eerily they stand,
While through them flit their ghosts—to wit,
   The Monk with the Red Hand,
The Eyeless Girl—an awful spook—
   To stop the boldest breath,
The boy that inked his copybook,
   And so got 'wopped' to death !

Call them not shams—from haunted Glamis
   To haunted Woodhouselea,
I mark in hosts the grisly ghosts
   I hear the fell Banshie !
I know the spectral dog that howls
   Before the death of Squires ;
In my 'Ghosts'-guide' addresses hide
   For Podmore and for Myers !

I see the Vampire climb the stairs
  From vaults below the church ;
And hark ! the Pirate's spectre swears !
  O Psychical Research,
Canst *thou* not hear what meets my ear,
  The viewless wheels that come ?
The wild Banshie that wails to thee ?
  The Drummer with his drum ?

O Haunted Homes of England,
  Though tenantless ye stand,
With none content to pay the rent,
  Through all the shadowy land,
Now, Science true will find in you
  A sympathetic perch,
And take you all, both Grange and Hall,
  For Psychical Research !

THE DISAPPOINTMENT

A House I took, and many a spook
    Was deemed to haunt that House,
I bade the glum Researchers come
    With Bogles to carouse.
That House I'd sought with anxious thought,
    'Twas old, 'twas dark as sin,
And *deeds of bale*, so ran the tale,
    Had oft been done therein.

Full many a child its mother wild,
    Men said, had strangled there,
Full many a sire, in heedless ire,
    Had slain his daughter fair!
'Twas rarely let: I can't forget
    A recent tenant's dread,
This widow lone had heard a moan
    Proceeding from her bed.

The tenants next were chiefly vexed
  By spectres grim and grey.
A Headless Ghost annoyed them most,
  And so they did not stay.
The next in turn saw corpse lights burn,
  And also a Banshie,
A spectral Hand they could not stand,
  And left the House to me.

Then came my friends for divers ends,
  Some curious, some afraid;
No direr pest disturbed their rest
  Than a neat chambermaid.
The grisly halls were gay with balls,
  One melancholy nook
Where ghosts *galore* were seen before
  Now yielded ne'er a spook.

When man and maid, all unafraid,
  'Sat out' upon the stairs,
No spectre dread, with feet of lead,
  Came past them unawares.

I know not why, but alway I
    Have found that it is so,
That when the glum Researchers come
    The brutes of bogeys—go !

TO THE GENTLE READER

'A French writer (whom I love well) speaks of three kinds of companions, —men, women, and books.'

SIR JOHN DAVYS.

THREE kinds of companions, men, women, and
    books,
Were enough, said the elderly Sage, for his ends.
And the women we deem that he chose for their
    looks,
And the men for their cellars: the books were
    his friends:
'Man delights me not,' often, 'nor woman,' but
    books
Are the best of good comrades in loneliest nooks.

For man will be wrangling—for woman will fret
About anything infinitesimal small:
Like the Sage in our Plato, I'm 'anxious to get
On the side '—on the sunnier side—'of a wall.'

F

Let the wind of the world toss the nations like
    rooks,
If only you 'll leave me at peace with my Books.

And which are my books? why, 'tis much as you
    please,
For, given 'tis a book, it can hardly be wrong,
And Bradshaw himself I can study with ease,
Though for choice I might call for a Sermon or
    Song;
And Locker on London, and Sala on Cooks,
'Tom Brown,' and Plotinus, they 're all of them
    Books.

There 's Fielding to lap one in currents of mirth;
There 's Herrick to sing of a flower or a fay;
Or good Maître Françoys to bring one to earth,
If Shelley or Coleridge have snatched one away:
There 's Müller on Speech, there is Gurney on
    Spooks,
There is Tylor on Totems, there 's all sorts of
    Books.

There's roaming in regions where every one's
      been,
Encounters where no one was ever before,
There's 'Leaves' from the Highlands we owe to
      the Queen,
There's Holly's and Leo's adventures in Kôr:
There's Tanner who dwelt with Pawnees and
      Chinooks,
You can cover a great deal of country in Books.

There are books, highly thought of, that nobody
      reads,
There is Geusius' dearly delectable tome
Of the Cannibal—he on his neighbour who
      feeds—
And in blood-red morocco 'tis bound, by Derome ;
There's Montaigne here (a Foppens), there's
      Roberts (on Flukes),
There's Elzevirs, Aldines, and Gryphius' Books.

There's Bunyan, there's Walton, in early editions,
There's many a quarto uncommonly rare ;

There's quaint old Quevedo adream with his
　　visions,
There's Johnson the portly, and Burton the spare ;
There's Boston of Ettrick, who preached of the
　　'Crooks
In the Lots' of us mortals, who bargain for Books.

There's Ruskin to keep one exclaiming 'What
　　next ?'
There's Browning to puzzle, and Gilbert to chaff,
And Marcus Aurelius to soothe one if vexed,
And good MARCUS TVAINUS to lend you a laugh ;
There be capital tomes that are filled with fly-
　　hooks,
And I've frequently found them the best kind of
　　Books.

THE SONNET

Poet, beware !   The sonnet's primrose path
   Is all too tempting for thy feet to tread.
   Not on this journey shalt thou earn thy bread,
Because the sated reader roars in wrath :
' Little indeed to say the singer hath,
   And little sense in all that he hath said ;
   Such rhymes are lightly writ but hardly read,
And naught but stubble is his aftermath ! '

Then shall he cast that bonny book of thine
   Where the extreme waste-paper basket gapes,
There shall thy futile fancies peak and pine,
   With other minor poets, pallid shapes,
Who come a long way short of the divine,
   Tormented souls of imitative apes.

THE TOURNAY OF THE HEROES

Ho, warders, cry a tournay ! ho, heralds, call the
    knights !
What gallant lance for old Romance 'gainst
    modern fiction fights ?
The lists are set, the Knights are met, I ween, a
    dread array,
St. Chad to shield, a stricken field shall we be-
    hold to-day !
First to the Northern barriers pricks Roland of
    Roncesvaux,
And by his side, in knightly pride, Wilfred of
    Ivanhoe,
The Templar rideth by his rein, two gallant foes
    were they ;
And proud to see, *le brave Bussy* his colours doth
    display.

Ready at need he comes with speed, William of
    Deloraine,
And Hereward the Wake himself is pricking o'er
    the plain.
The good knight of La Mancha's here, here is Sir
    Amyas Leigh,
And Eric of the gold hair, pride of Northern
    chivalry.
There shines the steel of Alan Breck, the sword
    of Athos shines,
Dalgetty on Gustavus rides along the marshalled
    lines,
With many a knight of sunny France the Cid
    has marched from Spain,
And Götz the Iron-handed leads the lances of
    Almain.

But who upon the Modern side are champions?
    With the sleeve
Adorned of his false lady-love, rides glorious
    David Grieve,

A bookseller sometime was he, in a provincial
    town,
But now before his iron mace go horse and rider
    down.
Ho, Robert Elsmere! count thy beads; lo,
    champion of the fray,
With brandished colt, comes Felix Holt, all of
    the Modern day.
And Silas Lapham's six-shooter is cocked: the
    Colonel's spry !
There spurs the wary Egoist, defiance in his
    eye ;
There Zola's ragged regiment comes, with dyna-
    mite in hand,
And Flaubert's crew of country doctors devastate
    the land.
On Robert Elsmere Friar Tuck falls with his
    quarter-staff,
Nom Dé ! to see the clerics fight might make the
    sourest laugh !
They meet, they shock, full many a knight is
    smitten on the crown,

So keep us good St. Geneviève, Umslopogaas is
    down !

About the mace of David Grieve his blood is
    flowing red,

Alas for ancient chivalry, *le brave Bussy* is sped !

Yet where the sombre Templar rides the Modern
    caitiffs fly,

The Mummer (of *The Mummer's Wife*) has got it
    in the eye,

From Felix Holt his patent Colt hath not averted
    fate,

And Silas Lapham's smitten fair, right through
    his gallant pate.

There Dan Deronda reels and falls, a hero sore
    surprised ;

Ha, Beauséant ! still may such fate befall the
    Circumcised !

The Egoist is flying fast from him of Ivanhoe :

Beneath the axe of Skalagrim fall prigs at every
    blow :

The ragged Zolaists have fled, screaming '*We are
    betrayed,*'

But loyal Alan Breck is shent, stabbed through
    the Stuart plaid ;
In sooth it is a grimly sight, so fast the heroes
    fall,
Three volumes fell could scarcely tell the fortunes
    of them all.
At length but two are left on ground, and David
    Grieve is one.
Ma foy, what deeds of derring-do that bookseller
    hath done !
The other, mark the giant frame, the great por-
    tentous fist !
'Tis Porthos !   David Grieve may call on Kuenen
    an he list.
The swords are crossed ; *Doublez, dégagez, vite !*
    great Porthos calls,
And David drops, that secret *botte* hath pierced
    his overalls !
And goodly Porthos, as of old the famed Or-
    thryades,
Raises the trophy of the fight, then falling on his
    knees,

He writes in gore upon his shield, 'Romance,
    Romance, has won!'
And blood-red on that stricken field goes down
    the angry sun.
Night falls upon the field of death, night on the
    darkling lea:
Oh send us such a tournay soon, and send me
    there to see!

BALLAD OF THE PHILANTHROPIST

POMONA Road and Gardens, N.,
Were pure as they were fair—
In other districts much I fear,
That vulgar language shocks the ear,
But brawling wives or noisy men
Were never heard of *there*.

No burglar fixed his dread abode
In that secure retreat,
There were no public-houses nigh,
But chapels low and churches high,
You might have thought Pomona Road
A quite ideal beat !

Yet that was not at all the view
Taken by B. 13.
That active and intelligent
Policeman deemed that he was meant

Profound detective deeds to do,
And that repose was mean.

Now there was nothing to detect
Pomona Road along—
None faked a cly, nor cracked a crib,
Nor prigged a wipe, nor told a fib,—
Minds cultivated and select
Slip rarely into wrong !

Thus bored to desolation went
The Peeler on his beat ;
He knew not Love, he did not care,
If Love be born on mountains bare ;
Nay, crime to punish, or prevent,
Was more than dalliance sweet !

The weary wanderer, day by day,
Was marked by Howard Fry—
A neighbouring philanthropist,
Who saw what that Policeman missed—
A sympathetic ' Well-a-day '
He 'd moan, and pipe his eye.

'What *can* I do,' asked Howard Fry,
'To soothe that brother's pain?
His glance when first we met was keen,
Most martial and erect his mien'
(What mien may mean, I know not I)
'But *he* must joy again.'

'I'll start on a career of crime,
I will,' said Howard Fry—
He spake and acted! Deeds of bale
(With which I do not stain my tale)
He wrought like mad time after time,
Yet wrought them blushfully.

And now when 'buses night by night
Were stopped, conductors slain,
When youths and men, and maids unwed,
Were stabbed or knocked upon the head,
Then B. 13 grew sternly bright,
And was himself again!

Pomona Road and Gardens, N.,
Are now a name of fear.

Commercial travellers flee in haste,
Revolvers girt about the waist
Are worn by city gentlemen
Who have their mansions near.

But B. 13 elated goes,
Detection in his eye ;
While Howard Fry does deeds of bale
(With which I do not stain my tale)
To lighten that Policeman's woes,
But does them blushfully.

MORAL

Such is Philanthropy, my friends,
Too often such her plan,
She shoots, and stabs, and robs, and flings
Bombs, and all sorts of horrid things.
Ah, not to serve her private ends,
But for the good of Man !

NEIGES D'ANTAN

G

IN ERCILDOUNE

In light of sunrise and sunsetting,
The long days lingered, in forgetting
That ever passion, keen to hold
What may not tarry, was of old
Beyond the doubtful stream whose flood
Runs red waist-high with slain men's blood.

Was beauty once a thing that died ?
Was pleasure never satisfied ?
Was rest still broken by the vain
Desire of action, bringing pain,
To die in vapid rest again ?
All this was quite forgotten, there
No winter brought us cold and care,
Nor spring gave promise unfulfilled,
Nor, with the heavy summer killed,
The languid days droop autumnwards.
So magical a season guards

The constant prime of a green June.
So slumbrous is the river's tune,
That knows no thunder of rushing rains,
Nor ever in the summer wanes,
Like waters of the summer-time
In lands far from the fairy clime.

Alas! no words can bring the bloom
Of Fairyland, the lost perfume.
The sweet low light, the magic air,
To minds of who have not been there:
Alas! no words, nor any spell
Can lull the heart that knows too well
The towers that by the river stand,
The lost fair world of Fairyland.

Ah, would that I had never been
The lover of the Fairy Queen.
Or would that I again might be
Asleep below the Eildon Tree,
And see her ride the forest way
As on that morning of the May!

Or would that through the little town,
The grey old place of Ercildoune,
And all along the sleepy street
The soft fall of the white deer's feet
Came, with the mystical command,
That I must back to Fairy Land!

FOR A ROSE'S SAKE

I LAVED my hands
   By the water-side,
With willow leaves
   My hands I dried.

The nightingale sang
   On the bough of a tree,
Sing, sweet nightingale,
   It is well with thee.

Thou hast heart's delight,
   I have sad heart's sorrow,
For a false false maid
   That will wed to-morrow.

It is all for a rose
   That I gave her not,

And I would that it grew
  In the garden plot,

And I would the rose-tree
  Were still to set,
That my love Marie
  Might love me yet!

THE BRIGAND'S GRAVE

MODERN GREEK

THE moon came up above the hill,
 The sun went down the sea,
 Go, maids, and draw the well-water,
 But, lad, come here to me.

Gird on my jack, and my old sword,
 For I have never a son,
And you must be the chief of all
 When I am dead and gone.

But you must take my old broadsword,
 And cut the green boughs of the tree,
And strew the green boughs on the ground,
 To make a soft death-bed for me.

And you must bring the holy priest,
 That I may sainèd be,

For I have lived a roving life
   Fifty years under the greenwood tree.

And you shall make a grave for me,
   And dig it deep and wide,
That I may turn about and dream
   With my old gun by my side.

And leave a window to the east
   And the swallows will bring the spring,
And all the merry month of May
   The nightingales will sing.'

THE NEW-LIVERIED YEAR

FROM CHARLES D'ORLÉANS

THE year has changed his mantle cold
    Of wind, of rain, of bitter air,
And he goes clad in cloth of gold
    Of laughing suns and season fair ;
No bird or beast of wood or wold
    But doth in cry or song declare
'The year has changed his mantle cold
All founts, all rivers seaward rolled
      Their pleasant summer livery wear
      With silver studs on broidered vair,
The world puts off its raiment old,
The year has changed his mantle cold.

MORE STRONG THAN DEATH

FROM VICTOR HUGO

Since I have set my lips to your full cup, my
    sweet,
Since I my pallid face between your hands have
    laid,
Since I have known your soul and all the bloom
    of it,
And all the perfume rare, now buried in the shade,

Since it was given to me to hear one happy while
The words wherein your heart spoke all its
    mysteries,
Since I have seen you weep, and since I have seen
    you smile,
Your lips upon my lips, and your eyes upon my
    eyes ;

Since I have known above my forehead glance
and gleam,
A ray, a single ray of your star veiled always,
Since I have felt the fall upon my lifetime's
stream
Of one rose-petal plucked from the roses of your
days ;   .

I now am bold to say to the swift-changing
hours,
Pass, pass upon your way, for I grow never old.
Fleet to the dark abyss with all your fading
flowers,
One rose that none may pluck within my heart I
hold.

Your flying wings may smite, but they can never
spill
The cup fulfilled of love from which my lips are wet,
My heart has far more fire than you have frost
to chill.
My soul more love than you can make my soul
forget.

SILENTIA LUNAE

FROM RONSARD

HIDE this one night thy crescent, kindly Moon,
  So shall Endymion faithful prove, and rest
  Loving and unawakened on thy breast;
So shall no foul enchanter importune
Thy quiet course, for now the night is boon,
  And through the friendly night unseen I
    fare
  Who dread the face of foemen unaware,
And watch of hostile spies in the bright noon.

Thou know'st, O Moon, the bitter power of Love.
'Tis told how shepherd Pan found ways to move
  With a small gift thy heart; and of your
    grace,
Sweet stars, be kind to this not alien fire,
Because on earth ye did not scorn desire,
  Bethink ye, now ye hold your heavenly place.

HIS LADY'S TOMB

FROM RONSARD

As in the gardens, all through May, the Rose,
　　Lovely, and young, and rich apparelled,
　　Makes sunrise jealous of her rosy red,
When dawn upon the dew of dawning glows;
　　Graces and Loves within her breast repose,
　　　　The woods are faint with the sweet odour
　　　　　　shed,
　　　　Till rains and heavy suns have smitten dead
The languid flower and the loose leaves unclose,—

So this, the perfect beauty of our days,
When heaven and earth were vocal of her praise,
　　　　The fates have slain, and her sweet soul
　　　　　　reposes:
And tears I bring, and sighs, and on her tomb
Pour milk, and scatter buds of many a bloom,
　　　　That, dead as living, Rose may be with roses.

THE POET'S APOLOGY

No, the Muse has gone away,
Does not haunt me much to-day.
Everything she had to say
       Has been said!
'Twas not much at any time
She could hitch into a rhyme,
Never was the Muse sublime
       Who has fled!

Any one who takes her in
May observe she's rather thin;
Little more than bone and skin
       Is the Muse;
Scanty sacrifice she won
When her very best she'd done,
And at her they poked their fun,
       In Reviews.

'Rhymes,' in truth, 'are stubborn things.'
And to Rhyme she clung, and clings,
But whatever song she sings
      Scarcely sells.
If her tone be grave, they say
'Give us something rather gay.'
If she's skittish, then they pray
      'Something else!'

Much she loved, for wading shod,
To go forth with line and rod,
Loved the heather, and the sod,
      Loved to rest
On the crystal river's brim
Where she saw the fishes swim,
And she heard the thrushes' hymn,
      By the Test!

She, whatever way she went,
Friendly was and innocent,
Little need the Bard repent
      Of her lay.

Of the babble and the rhyme,
And the imitative chime
That amused him on a time,—
    Now he's grey.

NOTES

NOTES

Page 1.

Jeanne d'Arc is said to have led a Scottish force at Lagny, when she defeated the Burgundian, Franquet d'Arras. A Scottish artist painted her banner; he was a James Polwarth, or a Hume of Polwarth, according to a conjecture of Mr. Hill Burton's. A monk of Dunfermline, who continued Fordun's Chronicle, avers that he was with the Maiden in her campaigns, and at her martyrdom. He calls her *Puella a spiritu sancto excitata*. Unluckily his manuscript breaks off in the middle of a sentence. This manuscript is No. viii. in the Fairfax Collection at the Bodleian; despite the opinion of Lord Fairfax (1650), it is not the original. The author, as Mr. W. F. Skene has shown, was possibly Maurice Buchanan, a great-nephew of Sir John Stewart of Dernley, slain at Rouvray, Feb. 12, 1429. How a

Scottish clerk came to be at the martyrdom in Rouen is unexplained, unless he was present in disguise. At her trial, Jeanne said that she had only once seen her own portrait : it was in the hands of a Scottish archer. The story of the white dove which passed from her lips as they opened to her last cry of *Jesus!* was reported at the trial for her Rehabilitation (1450-56).

Page 2.

One of that name.

Two archers of the name of Lang, Lain, or Laing were in the French service about 1507. See the book on the Scottish Guard, by Father Forbes Leith, S.J.

Thy Church unto the Maid denies.

These verses were written, curiously enough, the day before the Maiden was raised to the rank of 'Venerable,' a step towards her canonisation, which, we trust, will not be long delayed. It is not easy for any one to understand the whole miracle of the life and death of Jeanne d'Arc, and the absolutely unparalleled grandeur and charm of her character, without studying the full records of both her trials, as collected and published by M. Quicherat, for the Société de l'Histoire de France.

Page 4.

How they held the Bass.

This story is versified from the account in *Memoirs of the Rev. John Blackader*, by Andrew Crichton, Minister of the Gospel. Second Edition. Edinburgh, 1826. Dunbar was retained as a prisoner, when negotiations for surrender, in 1691, were broken off by Middleton's return with supplies. Halyburton was, it seems, captured later, and only escaped hanging by virtue of the terms extorted by Middleton. Patrick Walker tells the tale of Peden and the girl. Wodrow, in his *Analecta*, has the story of the Angel, or other shining spiritual presence, which is removed from its context in the ballad. The sufferings from weak beer are quoted in Mr. Blackader's Memoirs. Mitchell was the undeniably brave Covenanter who shot at Sharp, and hit the Bishop of the Orkneys. He was tortured, and, by an act of perjury (probably unconscious) on the part of Lauderdale, was hanged. The sentiments of the poem are such as an old cavalier, surviving to 1743, might have entertained. 'Wullie Wanbeard' is a Jacobite name for the Prince of Orange. perhaps invented only by the post-Jacobite sentiment of the early nineteenth century.

Page 44.

Rousseau's delight.

The *pervenche*, or periwinkle.

Page 64.

One of the college bells of St. Salvator, mentioned by Ferguson, is called 'Kate Kennedy'; the heroine is unknown, but Bishop Kennedy founded the **College.** ' Kate Kennedy's Day ' was a kind of carnival, **probably** a survival from that festivity.

Page 77.

The Disappointment.

As a matter of fact the Haunted House Committee of the Society for Psychical Research have never succeeded in seeing a ghost.

Printed by T. and A. CONSTABLE, Printers to Her Majesty, at the Edinburgh University Press.